Milo and Georgie

To Dario and Oakland, for always looking
on the bright side, no matter what life hands us — B.G.

To Sam and Lucy — J.B.

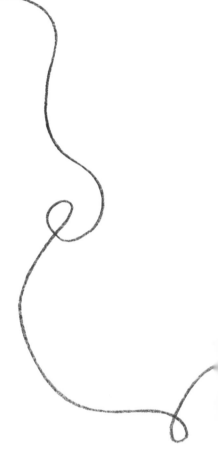

Owlkids Books acknowledges the financial support of the Canada Council for the Arts, the Ontario Arts
Council, the Government of Canada through the Canada Book Fund (CBF) and the Government of Ontario
through the Ontario Media Development Corporation's Book Initiative for our publishing activities.

Published in Canada by
Owlkids Books Inc.
10 Lower Spadina Avenue
Toronto, ON M5V 2Z2

Published in the United States by
Owlkids Books Inc.
1700 Fourth Street
Berkeley, CA 94710

Library and Archives Canada Cataloguing in Publication

Galbraith, Bree, 1981-, author
      Milo and Georgie / written by Bree Galbraith ; illustrated
by Josée Bisaillon.

ISBN 978-1-77147-170-1 (hardback)

      I. Bisaillon, Josée, 1982-, illustrator II. Title.

PS8613.A4592M55 2017   jC813'.6   C2016-904286-3

Library of Congress Control Number: 2016946650

The artwork in this book was rendered in watercolor, collage and digital illustration.
Edited by: Karen Li
Designed by: Barb Kelly

ONTARIO ARTS COUNCIL
CONSEIL DES ARTS DE L'ONTARIO
an Ontario government agency
un organisme du gouvernement de l'Ontario

Canada Council
for the Arts

Conseil des Arts
du Canada

Canadä

Manufactured in Shenzhen, Guangdong, China, in November 2016, by WKT Co. Ltd.
Job #16CB1345

A   B   C   D   E   F

 Publisher of Chirp, chickaDEE and OWL
www.owlkidsbooks.com   Owlkids Books is a division of  Bayard
CANADA

Milo and Georgie

Written by Bree Galbraith

Illustrated by Josée Bisaillon

Owlkids Books

Just as school ended for the year, Milo's mom got a new job. She took him and his sister, Georgie, out for ice cream to celebrate. But Milo didn't enjoy one bite because his mom told them there was something special about her job.

"It's in a new city," she explained. "We're moving in one month."

Milo put down his double-decker ice cream. "If we move, I will never be happy again," he told her. "I will never smile again, never laugh, and never eat ice cream."

Georgie didn't seem to mind. "Don't worry, Mom," she said. "I'll eat ice cream no matter where we go."

In the weeks that followed, Milo stayed out of the house. He went to the park and played baseball for the last time ever.

He threw his last pitch.

He hit his last home run.

At the age of eight and a half, Milo had retired from having fun.

Then came the big day. The family arrived at their new home.

"I hate it," said Milo. "It smells like other people's cooking. And I can hear the cars go by even with the windows closed."

"I love it," said Georgie. "We get to share a room!"

Milo and Georgie were introduced to their new babysitter, Mrs. Davies. Milo didn't like the taste of her cookies, and her lemonade was sour.

The first time Mrs. Davies looked after them, she fell asleep knitting. Milo watched TV all day while Georgie roamed around the house.

"I knew it!" said Milo. "There is nothing to do here. We should never have moved."

They didn't go out that day, or the next, or even the day after that. Milo turned up the TV so that he didn't have to hear Mrs. Davies snore—or listen to Georgie beg. "Please take me outside, Milo. I'll be super good."

Finally, Milo gave in.

When Mrs. Davies was sound asleep, Milo took the biggest ball of yarn he could find.

"Go outside. You'll see," he said, double-knotting the string around Georgie's middle. "This is the most awful place on earth."

He told Georgie he would tug twice on the string when she had to come home. "No later than four-thirty, when Mom gets back."

Milo closed the door carefully behind his sister and settled in with a glass of sour lemonade.

Weeks passed as Georgie explored the neighborhood.
On cool days, she came back with pink cheeks after running around with the neighborhood dogs.
On hot days, she came back soaked from a water fight or covered in "gelato"—something she claimed was even better than ice cream.

At three o'clock, one especially hot summer day, Milo tugged twice on the string. Ten minutes passed and Georgie hadn't returned. Milo tugged twice more. He waited and he waited, but no Georgie.

Milo paced back and forth. Their mother would be home soon.

He tied his end of the string to the door handle and hurried outside.

Milo squinted. He hadn't been outside in weeks.
As he followed the string, he was almost run over
by a pack of dogs.

"Watch out, my friend," said the dog walker.
"Are you lost? I don't think I've seen you around
here before."

"I'm looking for my sister," Milo said,
holding up the string.

"Georgie? Why didn't you say so! We can
help you find her!" She handed Milo a leash,
and the dog on the end gave him a friendly lick.

Half a block later, they passed a pizza parlor. Milo's stomach growled loudly. The chef looked at the string. "Where's Georgie?"

The dog walker piped up. "She's missing, Carl. The string must have broken."

Carl handed Milo a giant slice of pepperoni pizza. "Eat up, my friend," he told Milo with a wink. Then he placed a CLOSED sign in the window and joined the search.

Not one minute later, Milo was joined by a little
old man who said Georgie helped carry his groceries.
Then a noodle delivery guy, a letter carrier, two
break-dancers, and a gardener.

When everyone turned the corner, they met a baseball
team. Georgie had told them that Milo was "the best
baseball player in the world before he stopped having fun."

"We're looking for a shortstop, if you ever come out of
retirement," said the captain, tossing Milo a ball.

A long block later, Milo came to the end of the string. He looked at all the worried people gathered around him—people from Georgie's suppertime stories. Suddenly, he had an idea.

"Gelato!" he yelled. "What is gelato, and where can I get some?"

Milo followed the group through the streets, helping the old man keep up with the crowd. When they reached the gelateria, everyone let out a huge cry: "Georgie!"

"Milo!" she squealed. "This was supposed to be for you, but the string broke, and I couldn't remember how to get back home."

Georgie held up a cone. "I wanted you to be happy again."

Milo looked at Georgie and then at all
the people who had helped him find her.
"I am happy, Georgie," he told her. And for the
first time since they had moved, he really was!
     Milo untied his sister and held her hand.
"Now, let's go home."